Just in Time!

by Judith Stamper

Illustrated by
Duendes Del Sur

SCHOLASTIC INC.

New York   Toronto   London   Auckland   Sydney
Mexico City   New Delhi   Hong Kong

A special thanks to the JumpStart Software Team: Diana Rathe Pray, Bernadette Gonzalez, Shawna Meek, Stacy Dale, Marcela Cabrera, Diane Chang, Tom Klein, Jennifer Bradley, Linda Tomarchio, Stephanie Wise, Eileen Moskowitz, Irene Lane, Anna Bunyik, and Amanda Smith.

ISBN 0-439-16447-8

12 11 10 9 8 7 6   3 4 5/0
Printed in U.S.A.   23
                        First Scholastic printing, May 2000

Chapter 1

Bright and early, the JumpStart gang came to school.

"The JumpStart Science Fair is tonight at **6 o'clock**," said Eleanor. "I'm so excited!"

"Over here," called Frankie. "We have a lot of work to do setting up for the fair. No bones about it!"

"I want to see the volcano!" said Casey.

The kids began to set up for the fair.

"Look at this ant farm," said CJ.

"Yuck! A snake!" Kisha squealed.

"What happens if I pour this into the volcano?" asked Casey.

"Stop!" Frankie yelled. "It will explode!"

"Casey!" said Eleanor. "You have to think before you act!"

All morning the JumpStart gang kept working. Suddenly, Edison let out a yell.

"Yikes! Look up in the sky!"

A big hot-air balloon was floating down toward the school.

Hopsalot came in for a landing and hopped out of the basket.

"Check out my science project," he said proudly.

Hopsalot showed off his balloon.
Everyone loved his project.

Soon the gang went back to work. But not
Casey. He played with the balloon.
I wonder what this does, he said to himself.

Suddenly, a voice cried, "Whoa! Help! Up here!" Casey was floating in the sky!

"My friend!" cried Kisha.

"And my balloon!" cried Hopsalot.

"To the ship," Frankie called out. "We can save him!"

Chapter 2

Frankie took charge as captain of the ship.
"Eleanor and Kisha," he said. "Look at the map.
Hopsalot, check the wind. CJ and Edison, cast off!"
"We have to save Casey and I need my balloon
back!" said Hopsalot. "It's **12 o'clock** now. The fair
starts in just six hours."

An hour later, CJ climbed up the mast. "Hang on, Casey," he called. "We're on our way!"

"Hang on yourself, CJ!" yelled Edison.

"What's for lunch?" asked Kisha. "It's **1 o'clock** now and I'm starving!"

The ship followed Casey as his balloon raced across the sky.

"I think he's headed for Jungle Island," said Eleanor.

"Full speed ahead, mates!" Frankie called out.

"Jumping gerbils!" said Hopsalot. "It's **2 o'clock**. The fair starts in four hours! We'll never catch him in time!"

Just then, Eleanor cried, "Look! It's Jungle Island!"

Chapter 3

At **3 o'clock** the ship landed on Jungle Island. "Spread out and search," said Frankie. "Let's meet back here in one hour."

The friends looked all over the
island. . . .
   Up a tree . . .
   by the lake . . .
   and along the river . . .

They met again at **4 o'clock**.
"Where could he be?" Kisha asked.
"Ouch!" Frankie yelled.
They all looked up. It was Casey caught in a tree!

The gang worked together to get Casey down. At last, Casey and the balloon were out of the tree.

"Casey," Eleanor scolded. "You scared us! You know you need to think before you act!"

"I've learned my lesson," said Casey.

"Yikes! It's **5 o'clock**!" said Hopsalot. "Time to fly. The fair starts in one hour! I'll meet you there!"

Hopsalot got to the fair by **6 o'clock**.
The judges checked out his project.
"What a great hot-air balloon!" said one judge.

The rest of the gang arrived at the fair soon after. Casey didn't touch anything — not even the volcano!

"It's time to announce the winner," called the judges. "First prize goes to . . ."

"... Hopsalot and his hot-air balloon!"
Hopsalot hopped so high that he dropped his
prize. But Casey caught it ... just in time!